Cave-baby and the Mammoth

ReadZone Books Limited

First published in this edition 2015

© in this edition ReadZone Books Limited 2015
© in text Vivian French 2005
© in illustrations Lisa Williams 2005

Vivian French has asserted her right under the Copyright Designs and Patents Act 1988 to be identified as the author of this work.

Lisa Williams has asserted her right under the Copyright Designs and Patents Act 1988 to be identified as the illustrator of this work.

Every attempt has been made by the Publisher to secure appropriate permissions for material reproduced in this book. If there has been any oversight we will be happy to rectify the situation in future editions or reprints. Written submissions should be made to the Publisher.

British Library Cataloguing in Publication Data (CIP) is available for this title.

Printed in Malta by Melita Press.

ISBN 978 1 78322 126 4

Visit our website: www.readzonebooks.com

Cave-baby and the Mammoth

Vivian French
and Lisa Williams

"Waah!" wailed Cave-baby.
"Ssh!" said Cave-dad.

"Waah!" screamed
Cave-baby.

Thump! Thump!

"Mammoth!" shouted Cave-dad.

"Run!" shouted Cave-mum.

"Waah!" screeched Cave-baby.

THUMP! THUMP!

"WAAH!" screeched Cave-baby.

23

"CLEVER baby!" said
Cave-mum.
"Goo," said Cave-baby.

Did you enjoy this book?

Look out for more *Robins* titles –
first stories in only 50 words